THIS WHERE'S WALDO? BOOK BELONGS TO:

AGSTiN Alexander
Herriott – reece – DANlop

HEY, WALDO FANS! FIVE INTREPID TRAVELERS
ARE LOST IN EVERY SCENE! CAN YOU FIND THEM?

ODLAW    WIZARD
         WHITEBEARD    WENDA    WOOF    WALDO

AND IN EVERY SCENE, THE TRAVELERS
HAVE EACH LOST SOMETHING PRECIOUS!
CAN YOU FIND THESE ITEMS TOO?

WALDO'S KEY    WOOF'S BONE    WENDA'S CAMERA

WIZARD WHITEBEARD'S SCROLL    ODLAW'S BINOCULARS

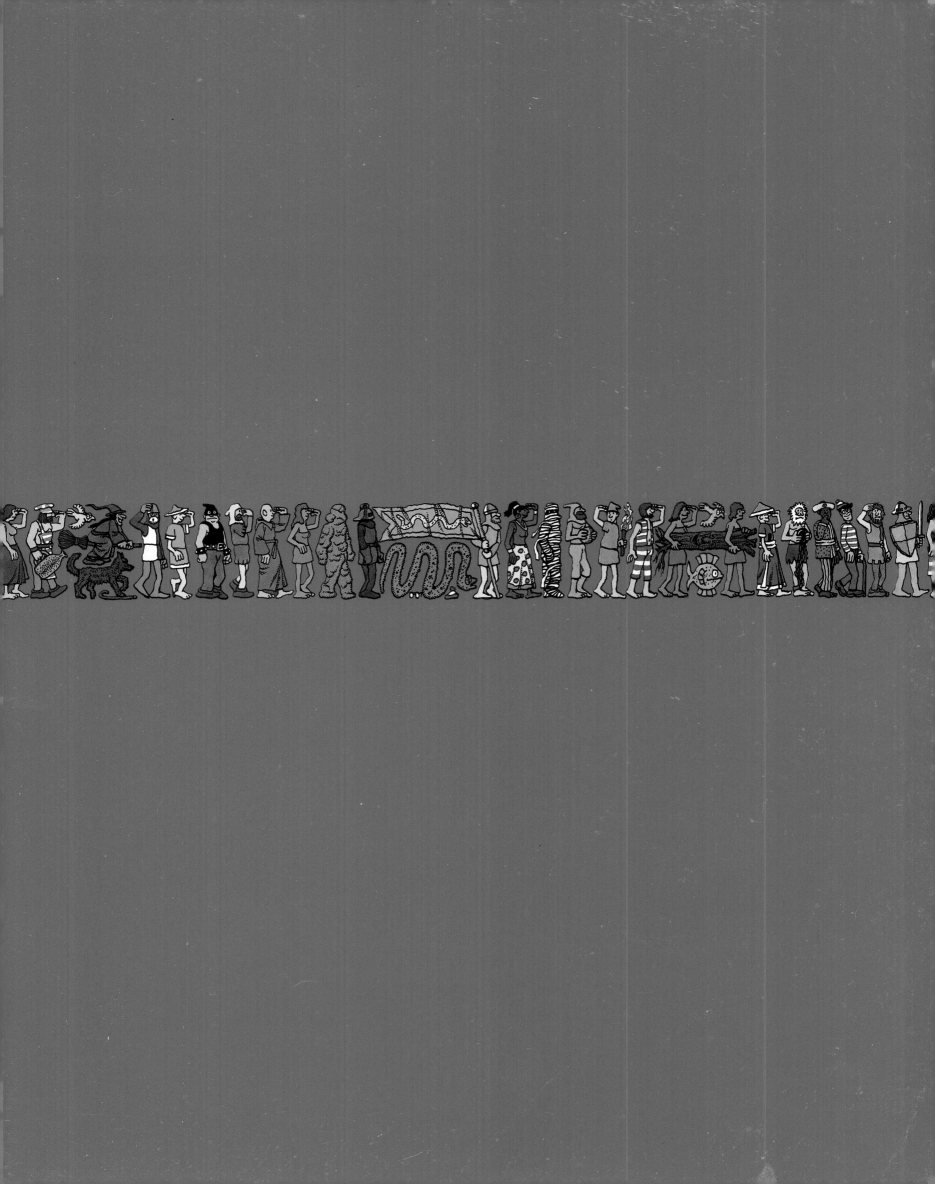

For everyone who has helped me,
especially Bryn, David Bennett, David,
Matthew, Sarah, Sebastian, and Steve.

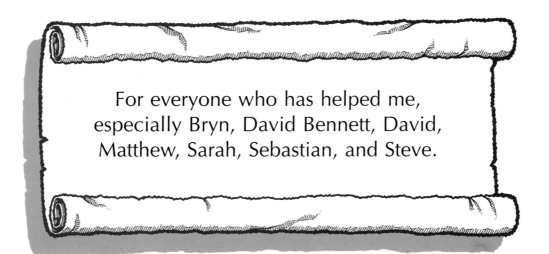

Copyright © 1989 by Martin Handford

First U.S. paperback edition 2007

The Library of Congress has cataloged the hardcover edition as follows:
Handford, Martin
[Great Waldo Search]
Where's Waldo?: the fantastic journey / Martin Handford, [author and illustrator].—2nd U.S. ed.
p.     cm.
Summary: The reader tries to follow Waldo as he embarks on a fantastic journey among the Gobbling Gluttons, the Battling
Monks, the Deep-sea Divers, the Underground Hunters, and the Land of Waldos in search of a special scroll.
ISBN 978-0-7636-0309-0 (hardcover)
[1. Voyages and travels—Fiction. 2. Humorous stories. 3. Picture puzzles.] I. Title.
PZ7.H1918Whd    1997
[Fic]—dc21    97-13735

ISBN 978-0-7636-3500-8 (paperback)

2 4 6 8 10 9 7 5 3 1

Printed in China

This book was typeset in Optima.
The illustrations were done in watercolor and water-based ink.

Candlewick Press
2067 Massachusetts Avenue
Cambridge, Massachusetts 02140

visit us at www.candlewick.com

# WHERE'S WALDO? THE FANTASTIC JOURNEY

## MARTIN HANDFORD

CANDLEWICK PRESS
CAMBRIDGE, MASSACHUSETTS

# THE GOBBLING GLUTTONS

ONCE UPON A TIME, WALDO EMBARKED UPON A FANTASTIC JOURNEY. FIRST, AMONG A THRONG OF GOBBLING GLUTTONS, HE MET WIZARD WHITEBEARD, WHO COMMANDED HIM TO FIND A SCROLL AND THEN TO FIND ANOTHER AT EVERY STAGE OF HIS JOURNEY. FOR WHEN HE HAD FOUND 12 SCROLLS, HE WOULD UNDERSTAND THE TRUTH ABOUT HIMSELF.

IN EVERY PICTURE FIND WALDO, WOOF (BUT ALL YOU CAN SEE IS HIS TAIL), WENDA, WIZARD WHITEBEARD, ODLAW, AND THE SCROLL. THEN FIND WALDO'S KEY, WOOF'S BONE (IN THIS SCENE IT'S THE BONE THAT'S NEAREST TO HIS TAIL), WENDA'S CAMERA, AND ODLAW'S BINOCULARS.

THERE ARE ALSO 25 WALDO-WATCHERS, EACH OF WHOM APPEARS ONLY ONCE SOMEWHERE IN THE FOLLOWING 12 PICTURES. AND ONE MORE THING! CAN YOU FIND ANOTHER CHARACTER, NOT SHOWN BELOW, WHO APPEARS ONCE IN EVERY PICTURE EXCEPT THE LAST?

# THE BATTLING MONKS

THEN WALDO AND WIZARD WHITEBEARD CAME TO THE PLACE WHERE THE INVISIBLE MONKS OF FIRE FOUGHT THE MONKS OF WATER. AND AS WALDO SEARCHED FOR THE SECOND SCROLL, HE SAW THAT MANY WALDOS HAD BEEN THIS WAY BEFORE. AND WHEN HE FOUND THE SCROLL, IT WAS TIME TO CONTINUE WITH HIS JOURNEY.

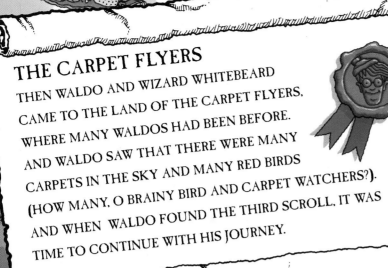

# THE CARPET FLYERS

THEN WALDO AND WIZARD WHITEBEARD
CAME TO THE LAND OF THE CARPET FLYERS,
WHERE MANY WALDOS HAD BEEN BEFORE.
AND WALDO SAW THAT THERE WERE MANY
CARPETS IN THE SKY AND MANY RED BIRDS
(HOW MANY, O BRAINY BIRD AND CARPET WATCHERS?).
AND WHEN WALDO FOUND THE THIRD SCROLL, IT WAS
TIME TO CONTINUE WITH HIS JOURNEY.

## THE GREAT BALLGAME PLAYERS

THEN WALDO AND WIZARD WHITEBEARD CAME TO THE PLAYING FIELD OF THE GREAT BALLGAME PLAYERS, WHERE MANY WALDOS HAD BEEN BEFORE. AND WALDO SAW THAT FOUR TEAMS WERE PLAYING AGAINST ONE ANOTHER (BUT WAS ANYONE WINNING? WHAT WAS THE SCORE? CAN YOU FIGURE OUT THE RULES?). THEN WALDO FOUND THE FOURTH SCROLL AND CONTINUED WITH HIS JOURNEY.

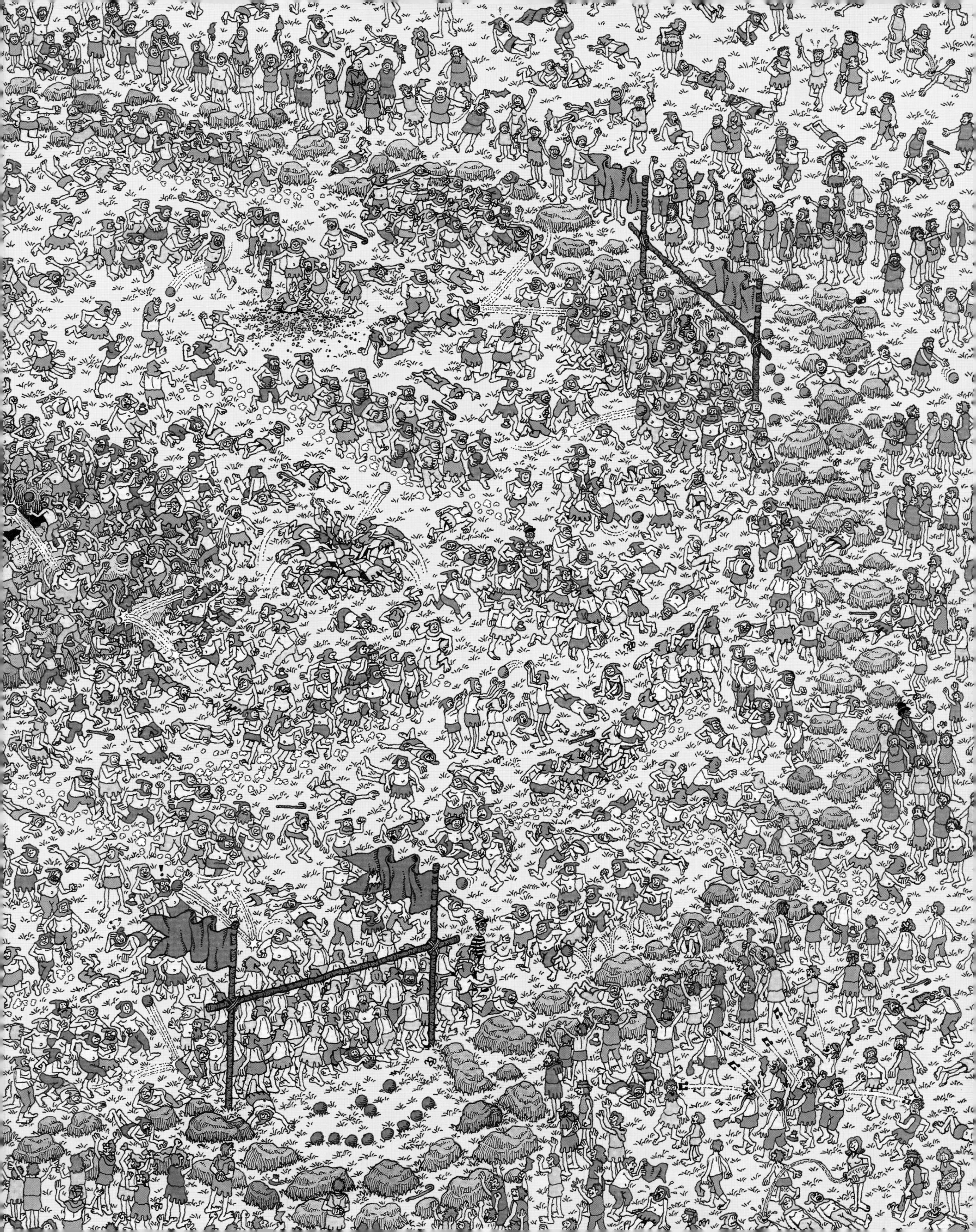

# THE FEROCIOUS RED DWARFS

THEN WALDO AND WIZARD WHITEBEARD CAME AMONG THE FEROCIOUS RED DWARFS, WHERE MANY WALDOS HAD BEEN BEFORE. AND THE DWARFS WERE ATTACKING THE MANY-COLORED SPEARMEN, CAUSING MIGHTY MAYHEM AND HORRID HAVOC. AND WALDO FOUND THE FIFTH SCROLL AND CONTINUED WITH HIS JOURNEY.

# THE NASTY NASTIES

THEN WALDO AND WIZARD WHITEBEARD CAME TO THE CASTLE OF THE NASTY NASTIES, WHERE MANY WALDOS HAD BEEN BEFORE. AND WHEREVER WALDO WALKED, THERE WAS A FEARFUL CLATTERING OF BONES (WOOF'S BONE IN THIS SCENE IS THE ONE NEAREST TO HIS TAIL) AND A FOUL SLURPING OF FILTHY FOOD. AND WALDO FOUND THE SIXTH SCROLL AND CONTINUED WITH HIS JOURNEY.

# THE FIGHTING FORESTERS

THEN WALDO AND WIZARD WHITEBEARD CAME AMONG THE FIGHTING FORESTERS, WHERE MANY WALDOS HAD BEEN BEFORE. AND IN THEIR BATTLE WITH THE EVIL BLACK KNIGHTS, THE FOREST WOMEN WERE AIDED BY THE ANIMALS, BY THE LIVING MUD, EVEN BY THE TREES THEMSELVES. AND WALDO FOUND THE SEVENTH SCROLL AND CONTINUED WITH HIS JOURNEY.

# THE DEEP-SEA DIVERS

THEN WALDO AND WIZARD WHITEBEARD CAME
TO THE WATERY WORLD OF THE DEEP-SEA
DIVERS, WHERE MANY WALDOS HAD BEEN
BEFORE. AND WALDO SEARCHED FOR THE EIGHTH
SCROLL AMONG THE MONSTERS OF THE DEEP, AMONG THE
MERMAIDS, FISHERMEN, AND FISH. AND WHEN HE FOUND IT,
IT WAS TIME TO CONTINUE WITH HIS JOURNEY.

THE KNIGHTS OF THE MAGIC FLAG

THEN WALDO AND WIZARD WHITEBEARD CAME TO A PLACE MORE CROWDED THAN ANY WALDO HAD SEEN BEFORE, WHERE TWO ARMIES WITH MANY MAGIC FLAGS WERE LOCKED IN COMBAT. AND WALDO SAW THAT MANY WALDOS HAD BEEN THIS WAY BEFORE. AND WHEN HE FOUND THE NINTH SCROLL, IT WAS TIME TO CONTINUE WITH HIS JOURNEY.

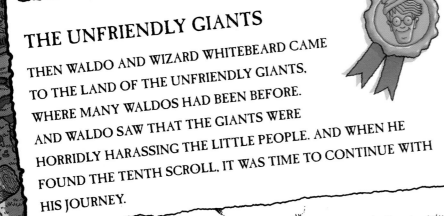

## THE UNFRIENDLY GIANTS

THEN WALDO AND WIZARD WHITEBEARD CAME TO THE LAND OF THE UNFRIENDLY GIANTS, WHERE MANY WALDOS HAD BEEN BEFORE. AND WALDO SAW THAT THE GIANTS WERE HORRIDLY HARASSING THE LITTLE PEOPLE. AND WHEN HE FOUND THE TENTH SCROLL, IT WAS TIME TO CONTINUE WITH HIS JOURNEY.

# THE UNDERGROUND HUNTERS

THEN WALDO AND WIZARD WHITEBEARD CAME AMONG THE UNDERGROUND HUNTERS, WHERE MANY WALDOS HAD BEEN BEFORE. THERE WAS MUCH MENACE IN THIS PLACE, AND A MULTITUDE OF MALEVOLENT MONSTERS. WALDO FOUND THE ELEVENTH SCROLL AND CONTINUED WITH HIS JOURNEY.

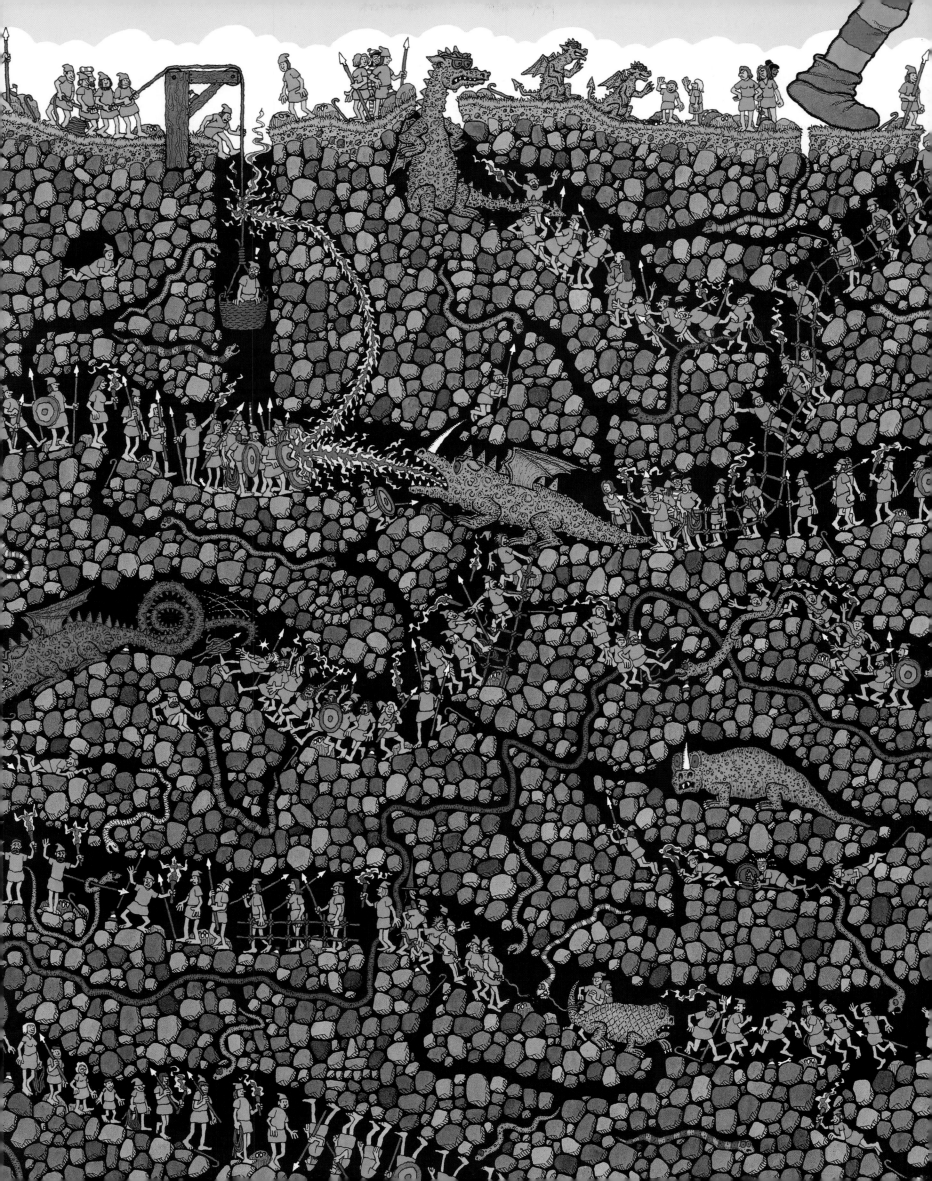

# THE LAND OF WALDOS

THEN WALDO FOUND THE TWELFTH SCROLL AND SAW THE TRUTH ABOUT HIMSELF, THAT HE WAS JUST ONE WALDO AMONG MANY. HE SAW, TOO, THAT WALDOS OFTEN LOSE THINGS, FOR HE HIMSELF HAD LOST ONE SHOE. AND AS HE LOOKED FOR HIS SHOE, HE DISCOVERED THAT WIZARD WHITEBEARD WAS NOT HIS ONLY FELLOW TRAVELER. THERE WERE NOW ELEVEN OTHERS—ONE FROM EVERY PLACE HE HAD BEEN TO— WHO HAD JOINED HIM ONE BY ONE ALONG THE WAY. SO NOW (O LOYAL FOLLOWERS OF WALDO!) FIND THE REAL WALDO AND HELP HIM FIND HIS MISSING SHOE. AND THERE, IN THE LAND OF WALDOS, MAY WALDO LIVE HAPPILY EVER AFTER.

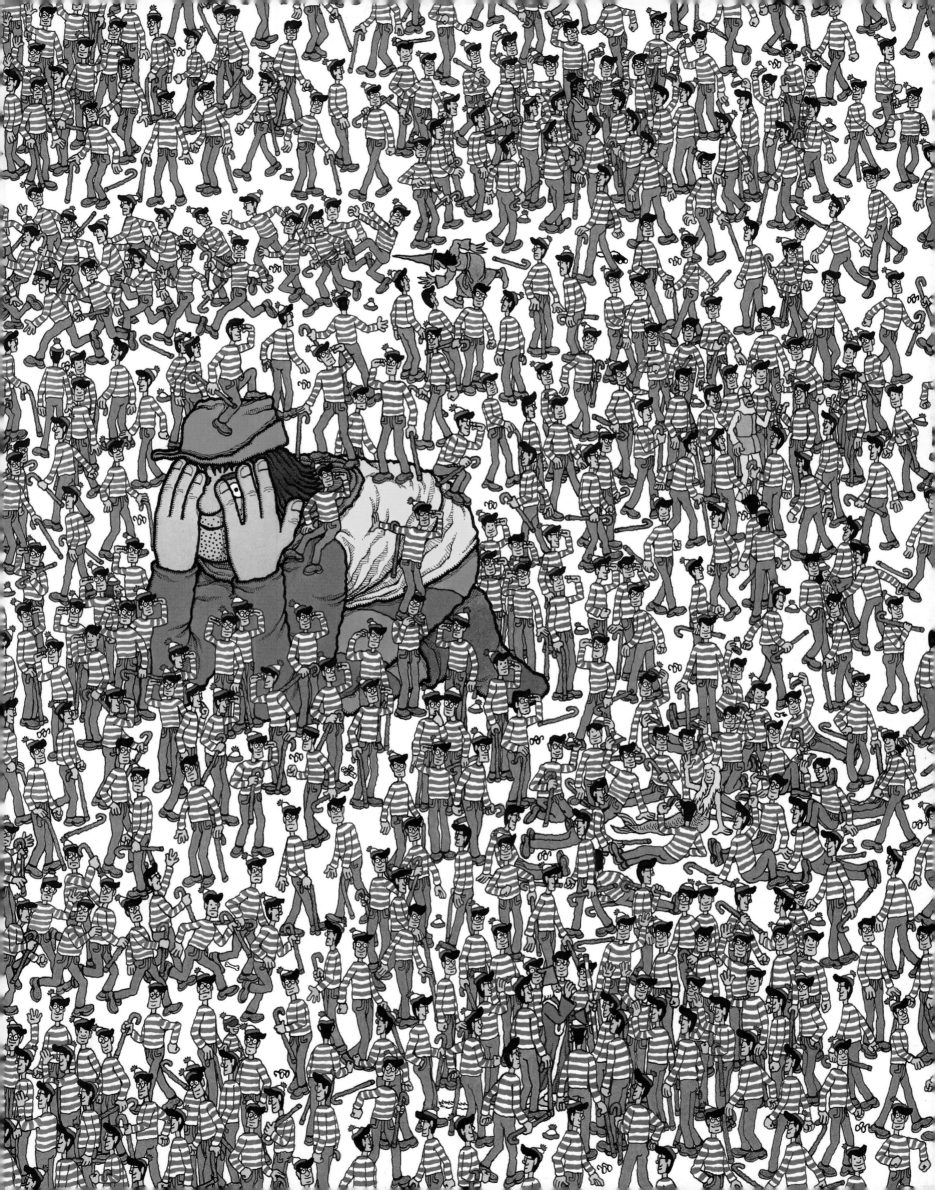

## THE GOBBLING GLUTTONS

- A strong waiter and a weak one
- Long-distance smells
- Unequal portions of pie
- A man who has had too much to drink
- People who are going the wrong way
- Very tough dishes
- An upside-down dish
- A very hot dinner
- Knights drinking through straws
- A clever drink pourer
- Giant sausages
- A custard fight
- An overloaded seat
- Beard-flavored soup
- Men pulling legs
- A painful spillage
- A poke in the eye
- A man tied up in spaghetti
- A knockout dish
- A man who has eaten too much
- A tall diner eating a tall dish
- An exploding pie
- A giant sausage breaking in half
- A smell traveling through two people

## THE CARPET FLYERS

- Two carpets on a collison course
- An overweight flyer
- A pedestrian crossing
- A carpet pinup
- Three hangers-on
- Flying hitchhikers
- An unsatisfied customer
- A used-carpet salesman
- A topsy-turvy tower
- A spiky crash
- Carpet cops and robbers
- A passing fruit thief
- Upside-down flyers
- A carpet repair shop
- Popular male and female flyers
- A flying tower
- A stair carpet
- Flying highwaymen
- Rich and poor flyers
- A carpet-breakdown rescue service
- Carpets flying on carpet flyers
- A carpet traffic policeman
- A flying carpet without a flyer

## THE BATTLING MONKS

- Two fire engines
- Hotfooted monks
- A bridge made of monks
- A smart-alecky monk
- A diving monk
- A scared statue
- Fire meeting water
- A snaking jet of water
- Chasers being chased
- A smug statue
- A snaking jet of flame
- A five-way washout
- A burning bridge
- Seven burning backsides
- Monks worshipping the Flowing Bucket of Water
- Monks shielding themselves from lava
- Thirteen trapped and extremely worried monks
- A monk seeing an oncoming jet of flame
- Monks worshipping the Mighty Erupting Volcano
- A very worried monk confronted by two opponents
- A burning hose
- Monks and lava pouring out of a volcano
- A chain of water
- Two monks accidentally attacking their brothers

## THE GREAT BALLGAME PLAYERS

- A three-way drink
- A row of hand-held banners
- A chase that goes around in circles
- A spectator surrounded by three rival supporters
- Players who can't see where they are going
- Two tall players versus short ones
- Seven awful singers
- A face made of balls
- Players who are digging for victory
- A face about to hit a fist
- A shot that breaks the woodwork
- A mob chasing a player backward
- A player chasing a mob
- Players pulling one anothers' hoods
- A flag with a hole in it
- A mob of players all holding balls
- A player heading a ball
- A player tripping over a rock
- A player punching a ball
- A spectator accidentally hitting two others
- A player sticking his tongue out at a mob
- A mouth pulled open by a beard
- A backside shot

## THE FEROCIOUS RED DWARFS

- A spear-breaking slingshot
- Two punches causing chain reactions
- Fat and thin spears and spearmen
- A spearman being knocked through a flag
- A collar made out of a shield
- A prison made of spears
- Tangled spears
- A devious disarmer
- Dwarfs disguised as spearmen
- A stickup machine
- A spearman trapped by his battle dress
- A sneaky spear bender
- An ax head causing headaches
- A dwarf who is on the wrong side
- Prankish target practice
- Opponents charging through each other
- A spearman running away from a spear
- A slingshot causing a chain reaction
- A sword cutting through a shield
- A spear hitting a spearman's shield
- A dwarf hiding up a spear
- Spearmen who have jumped out of their clothes
- A spear knocking off a dwarf's helmet

## THE NASTY NASTIES

- A vampire who is scared of ghosts
- Two vampire bears
- Vampires drinking through straws
- Gargoyle lovers
- An upside-down torture
- A baseball bat
- Three wolfmen
- A mummy who is coming undone
- A vampire mirror test
- A frightened skeleton
- Dog, cat, and mouse doorways
- Courting cats
- A ghoulish bowling game
- A gargoyle being poked in the eye
- An upside-down gargoyle
- Ghoulish flight controllers
- Three witches flying backward
- A witch losing her broomstick
- A broomstick flying a witch
- A ticklish torture
- A vampire about to get the chop
- A ghost train
- A vampire who doesn't fit his coffin
- A three-eyed, hooded torturer

## THE FIGHTING FORESTERS

- [ ] Three long legs
- [ ] A three-legged knight
- [ ] Knights being chopped down by a tree
- [ ] Two multiple knockouts
- [ ] A lazy lady
- [ ] A tree with a lot of puff
- [ ] Hardheaded women
- [ ] Attackers about to be attacked
- [ ] A strong woman and a weak one
- [ ] An easily frightened horse
- [ ] Eight pairs of upside-down feet
- [ ] Knights shooting arrows at knights
- [ ] An upside-down ladder
- [ ] Loving trees
- [ ] An upside-down trunk
- [ ] A two-headed unicorn
- [ ] A unicorn in a tree
- [ ] Trees with two faces
- [ ] Muddy mudslingers
- [ ] A tearful small tree
- [ ] Spears getting sharpened tips
- [ ] Trees branching out violently
- [ ] Stilts being chewed up

## THE DEEP-SEA DIVERS

- [ ] A two-headed fish
- [ ] A sword fight with a swordfish
- [ ] Fish fingers
- [ ] A seabed
- [ ] A fish face
- [ ] A catfish and a dogfish
- [ ] A jellyfish
- [ ] A fish with two tails
- [ ] A skate
- [ ] A sea lion
- [ ] Two fish-shaped formations
- [ ] Treacherous treasure
- [ ] Oyster beds
- [ ] Canned fish
- [ ] Flying fish
- [ ] Electric eels
- [ ] A deck of cards
- [ ] A bottle in a message
- [ ] A fake fin
- [ ] A backward mermaid
- [ ] A sea horse–drawn carriage
- [ ] A boat's compass
- [ ] A fish catching men
- [ ] An underwater beach scene
- [ ] Divers drawing on an angry sea monster

## THE KNIGHTS OF THE MAGIC FLAG

- [ ] Unfaithful royals
- [ ] A flag full of fists
- [ ] A game of tick-tack-toe
- [ ] A sword-fighting reindeer
- [ ] A man behind bars
- [ ] A mouse among lions
- [ ] Flags within a flag
- [ ] A tangle of tongues
- [ ] A zebra crossing
- [ ] An eagle dropping an eyeful
- [ ] A puffing spoilsport
- [ ] A battering-ram door key
- [ ] Snakes and ladders
- [ ] A flame-throwing dragon
- [ ] Diminishing desserts
- [ ] A crown thief
- [ ] A thirsty lion
- [ ] A weapons' imbalance
- [ ] A foot being tickled by a feather
- [ ] Some rude soldiers
- [ ] A surrendering reindeer
- [ ] A dog straining to get a bone
- [ ] A helmet with three eyes

## THE LAND OF WALDOS

- [ ] Waldos waving
- [ ] Waldos walking
- [ ] Waldos running
- [ ] Waldos sitting
- [ ] Waldos lying down
- [ ] Waldos sliding
- [ ] Waldos standing still
- [ ] Waldos smiling
- [ ] Waldos searching
- [ ] Waldos being chased
- [ ] Waldos giving the thumbs up
- [ ] Waldos looking frightened
- [ ] Waldos with bobble hats
- [ ] Waldos without bobble hats
- [ ] Waldos raising their bobble hats
- [ ] Waldos with walking sticks
- [ ] Waldos without walking sticks
- [ ] Waldos with glasses
- [ ] Waldos without glasses
- [ ] A Waldo on a hat
- [ ] A Waldo holding a wing
- [ ] Waldo

## THE UNDERGROUND HUNTERS

- [ ] A hunter about to put his foot in it
- [ ] Four frightened flames
- [ ] A snaky hat thief
- [ ] An underground traffic policeman
- [ ] Three surrendering flames
- [ ] A two-headed snake
- [ ] A snaky tickle
- [ ] A ridiculously long snake
- [ ] Three dragons wearing sunglasses
- [ ] A dragon that attacks with both ends
- [ ] Angry snake parents
- [ ] Five broken spears
- [ ] A monstrous bridge
- [ ] Five rock faces
- [ ] Upside-down hunters
- [ ] A snake that is trapped
- [ ] A very long ladder
- [ ] A torch setting fire to spears
- [ ] Hunters tripped by a tongue
- [ ] A hunter with an extra long spear
- [ ] Hunters about to collide
- [ ] Hunters going around in a circle
- [ ] A shocked tail puller

## THE UNFRIENDLY GIANTS

- [ ] Trappers about to be trapped
- [ ] A catapulted missile hitting people
- [ ] A hairy bird's nest
- [ ] Ducks out of water
- [ ] A mocking giant about to come unstuck
- [ ] Two broom trees
- [ ] Two giants who are out for the count
- [ ] Two windmill knockouts
- [ ] A polite giant about to get a headache
- [ ] A giant with a roof over his head
- [ ] Three people in a giant hood
- [ ] A battering-ram fist
- [ ] A house shaker
- [ ] A thumbtack trap
- [ ] A landslide of boulders
- [ ] Six people strapped inside giant belts
- [ ] People being swept off their feet
- [ ] People taking part in a board game
- [ ] Rope pullers being pulled
- [ ] Birds being disturbed by a giant
- [ ] Two game watchers slapping people
- [ ] Four shy ladies being flattered
- [ ] A powerful burst of pond water

## THE FANTASTIC JOURNEY

Did you find Waldo, his friends, and all the things that they had lost? Did you find the mystery character who appeared in every scene except the Land of Waldos? It may be difficult, but keep searching and eventually you'll find him—now that's a clue! And one last thing: Somewhere one of the Waldo-watchers lost the bobble from his hat. Can you find which one, and find the bobble?

# THE WHERE'S WALDO? COLLECTION

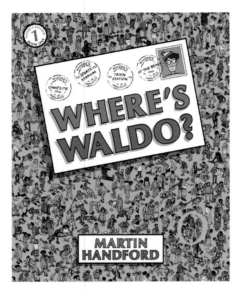

Down the road, over the sea, around the globe . . . Where's Waldo? on his worldwide adventures!

ISBN 978-0-7636-3498-8

Over thousands of years, past thousands of people . . . Where's Waldo? now!

ISBN 978-0-7636-3499-5

Once upon a mermaid, once upon a dragon . . . Where's Waldo? in the realms of fantasy!

ISBN 978-0-7636-3500-8

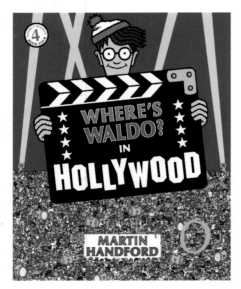

Lights, camera, action! Where's Waldo? behind the scenes!

ISBN 978-0-7636-3501-5

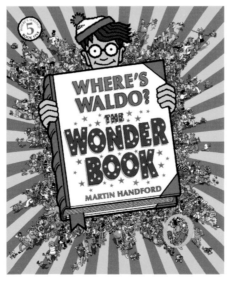

Stepping off the pages and into life . . . Where's Waldo? in lands full of wonder!

ISBN 978-0-7636-3502-2

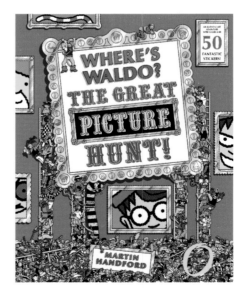

Pick a sticker, spot the difference, match the silhouettes . . . Where's Waldo? at the gallery!

ISBN 978-0-7636-3043-0

# Have you found all six Waldo books yet?